CONTENTS

Pedigree®

Published 2011. Pedigree Books Ltd, Beech Hill House,
Walnut Gardens, Exeter, Devon EX4 4DH
books@pedigreegroup.co.uk | www.pedigreebooks.com

THE SMURFS™

£7.99

Welcome to Smurf

Come and meet the Smurfs...

Papa Smurf

is the village chief. He was 542-years-old last Spring. He's a wise old Smurf and often saves the Smurfs from danger using his knowledge of alchemy.

Gutsy Smurf

is the most scrappy and brave-hearted in all of Smurfdom. He is the courageous problem-solver-in-chief who the other Smurfs turn to when they're in a tight spot.

Brainy Smurf

is Gutsy's only known adversary. He's the only Smurf to take everything in life seriously. Brainy spends his time putting the world to rights and he's a notorious tell-tale.

land

© Peyo

Clumsy Smurf is a walking, talking disaster. Whatever he does turns into a catastrophe. Whatever he tries to do always turns into an accident. And that's why no-one wants his help!

Grouchy Smurf always takes the opposite view to anything that anybody says or suggests. He always interrupts chats with negative comments, but deep down he has a heart of gold.

Smurfette was originally created by the horrible wizard Gargamel to cause trouble among the Smurfs. Papa Smurf used his alchemy knowledge to transform her into the charming Smurfette who melts the hearts of the others.

the Smurfs' friends and foes!

Gargamel

is a nasty, sneaky wizard who lives in a horrible cottage in the heart of the forest. He hates Smurfs and does everything within his power to capture them. He is also very stupid!

Azraël

the flea-bitten cat, is Gargamel's scapegoat. He follows the wizard everywhere, hoping his master will one day catch a tasty little Smurf. He is a potential menace to the Smurfs.

Grace Winslow

The pregnant wife of Patrick Winslow, who is eagerly awaiting the birth of her first baby. She loves her husband very much and is very proud of him and his achievements.

Patrick Winslow

A salesman for Anjelou Cosmetics, who has suddenly found himself promoted to Vice President of Marketing. It's a tough and demanding job, for an equally demanding boss. But he is confident!

Odd One Out!

All of these pictures of Papa Smurf look identical. But if you look closely, one of them is different. Circle the odd one out. **Answer on p76.**

1

2

3

4

5

6

7

8

10

Shadow Smurfs

Answer on p76.

Which one of these shadows is the exact silhouette of this picture of Clumsy? Circle your answer.

1

2

3

4

5

6

7

8

9

10

11

A very clumsy Smurf

Smurfs Story PART 1

There is a place that knows no sadness, where even feeling blue is a happy thing. It is a place inhabited by Smurfs, little blue beings, just three apples high.

This place lies deep in an enchanted forest, hidden away beyond a medieval village.

It is better known as the Smurf Village...

In the Smurf Village, where every Smurf plays their own special part, the Smurfs were preparing for the Blue Moon Festival. Farmer Smurf and Greedy Smurf had been riding on storks, collecting smurfberries for the party. Clumsy Smurf was late for the party and in his haste he knocked Handy Smurf off his step ladder, tripped over a barrel, dislodged all of Baker Smurf's pies and then stepped into one of the pies. He really was a very clumsy Smurf...

Meanwhile, away from the perfect life in Smurf Village, the evil wizard Gargamel and Azraël, his flea-bitten cat, were plotting against the Smurfs.

Gargamel was a tortured, power-hungry sorcerer who lived in a gnarled old castle. A single storm cloud hung continuously over the grim building.

"I'm not obsessed with Smurfs," snarled Gargamel. "I simply can't stop thinking about the miserable beasts every single minute of every single day. Because I need them.

"It is only by capturing the little wretches and extracting their happy blue essence that my magic will finally become invincible!

"I shall become the most powerful wizard in all of the world!" cackled Gargamel.

MUST.
HAVE.
SMURRRRFS.

15

Blue Moon Festival time was also when Papa Smurf created some Smurf magic. He needed to get the visionary potion just right so that he could look into the future. The magic was strongest at Blue Moon.

When he sprinkled the ingredients into a cauldron of boiling water, instead of the future showing happy, smiling Smurfs, smurfberries, singing and dancing, he saw a sinister dark cloud. The cloud cleared to reveal a medieval dungeon filled with scary looking machinery and terrified Smurfs locked in cages calling for help.

At the centre of the vision was an image of Clumsy. "Oh, Clumsy, what have you done?" asked Papa Smurf.

And at that moment Clumsy Smurf dashed into Papa Smurf's mushroom home and the draught from the open door blew away the visionary cloud.

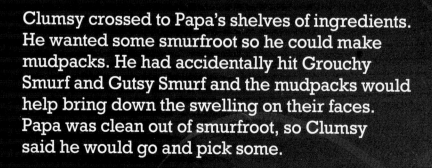

Clumsy crossed to Papa's shelves of ingredients. He wanted some smurfroot so he could make mudpacks. He had accidentally hit Grouchy Smurf and Gutsy Smurf and the mudpacks would help bring down the swelling on their faces. Papa was clean out of smurfroot, so Clumsy said he would go and pick some.

"No!" said Papa, remembering the vision. "Those fields are too close to Gargamel's castle. I'll get the smurfroot. You stay in the village and out of trouble."

Clumsy agreed, but a little later he still went to the lush forest to pick the smurfroot. As he congratulated himself on gathering so much smurfroot, the weeds behind him parted to reveal Azraël the cat and the wicked wizard Gargamel.

But Clumsy had spotted the wizard's shadow just in time and ran back to the village as fast as he could.

Gargamel and Azraël were right behind Clumsy, who accidentally led them straight through the invisibility shield and into the village. The Smurfs panicked and scattered into the forest to hide. Gargamel tried to catch Papa but his mushroom home was booby-trapped.

Papa Smurf was able to escape and follow the others. But Clumsy took a wrong path in the forest and was followed by Smurfette, Brainy, Grouchy, Gutsy and, at the rear, Papa.

They headed through a grotto towards the Forbidden Falls where Clumsy lost his balance.

The other Smurfs formed a chain to save Clumsy, but a hole appeared in the waterfall and they all fell through it after him.

Continued on p32

Brainy's Quiz

Use your knowledge of the film to answer the following questions.

1 Which of the Smurfs is the problem-solver?
Answer: *Brain*

2 How old is Papa Smurf?
Answer:

3 Why did Gargamel originally create Smurfette?
Answer:

4 Which of the Smurfs is a notorious tell-tale?
Answer:

5 What is Grouchy Smurf's heart made out of?
Answer:

6 Who or what is Gargamel?
Answer:

7 What did Papa Smurf do for Smurfette?
Answer: *Make her a real smurf*

8 What is Azraël?
Answer:

9 What is the name of the festival that the Smurfs are collecting berries for?
Answer: *blue moon*

10 Why does no-one want any help from Clumsy Smurf?
Answer:

11 Which TV station is at the press launch?
Answer:

12 Who is the human hero of the Smurf's latest adventure?
Answer:

13

What is the name of the company hosting a press event in the boathouse?
Answer:

14

Who owns the company hosting the press event?
Answer:

15

How did the Smurfs get to the boathouse in the first place?
Answer:

16

How many Smurfs land in New York's Central Park?
Answer: *6*

17

How old is Grace?
Answer:

18

What is Patrick's nickname for Odile?
Answer:

19

Why did the Smurfs chase after Patrick?
Answer:

20

What is the name of the castle in New York?
Answer:

Answers on p76

Five pieces are needed to complete this jigsaw. Use a pen or pencil to draw a line to connect the correct pieces with the blank spaces.

Answers on p76

© Peyo

23

Brainy Crossword

Using the clues, complete this Smurfs crossword.

Across

1. Charming female who melts hearts. (9)
3. A yellow taxi in New York. (3)
4. (and 11 across) An essential potion ingredient. (5, 4)
5. Where Patricks press event is being held. (9)
8. The colour of Smurfs, or a certain kind of moon. (4)
10. (see 2 down)
11. (see 4 across)
12. An accident prone Smurf. (6)

Down

1. A bird known for delivering babies. (6)
2. (and 10 across) The Smurfs village lies deep within this. (9, 6)
6. Little blue beings, three apples high. (6)
7. Time travel opening. (6)
9. Gargamels cat. (6)

Answers on p76.

Papa Smurf devised this testing wordsearch. The words listed at the bottom of the page are all hidden in the grid. They can be found in a straight line only, forwards or backwards, up or down, and diagonally. Draw a line through them as you find them.

E	Q	F	R	U	M	S	R	E	M	R	A	F	J	T
P	L	A	C	O	S	M	B	H	E	N	R	I	Z	M
A	Y	T	O	J	W	Q	A	G	S	D	F	F	G	F
T	P	O	S	U	V	I	R	Y	T	R	E	T	W	R
R	M	L	M	A	A	A	K	J	H	N	N	H	K	U
I	N	B	E	V	C	C	X	Z	Z	O	E	A	R	M
C	N	B	T	E	D	E	V	C	X	I	W	V	A	S
K	O	D	I	L	E	M	R	L	K	T	Y	E	P	Y
F	G	H	C	J	B	L	U	E	M	O	O	N	L	H
D	F	E	S	T	I	V	A	L	D	P	R	U	A	C
S	A	L	E	M	A	G	R	A	G	E	K	E	R	U
T	E	D	S	M	U	R	F	R	E	W	V	Q	T	O
F	R	U	M	S	Y	D	E	E	R	G	Y	L	N	R
T	C	R	U	E	L	L	A	D	O	D	I	L	E	G
A	N	J	E	L	O	U	U	I	O	P	P	O	C	B

Anjelou
Belvedere Castle
Blue Moon
Central Park
Cosmetics
Cruella DOdile
Farmer Smurf

Festival
Fifth Avenue
Gargamel
Grace
Greedy Smurf
Grouchy Smurf
Henri

New York
Odile
Patrick
Potion
Ted Smurf

Answers on p76.

How to draw a
Smurf

Using the grid lines as a guide, can you copy the picture of Grouchy Smurf into the space below? When you have finished, why not colour him in with your coloured pencils or crayons.

What goes where?

Clumsy Smurf has messed up this picture. Can you work out the correct order for the strips? Write the numbers into the boxes. The letters may also help, once in correct order they will complete the saying at the bottom...

?	?	?	?	?
1	2	3	4	5

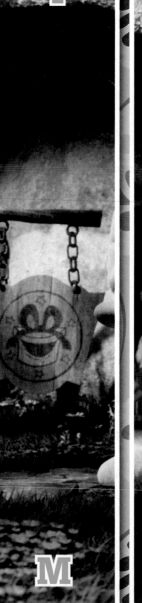

F	S	U	M	R

?	?	?	?	?	HAPPENS

Answers on p77

28

Box the Smurf!

Find a friend or two to play this game with you. Each takes a turn to join two dots using a pen or a pencil. When you have completed a box by joining the last two dots, write your initials in the completed box and have another go. For every square you win, award yourself a point. If your square also has a Smurfs face inside, award yourself an extra bonus point. The winner is the person with the most points. This page can be photocopied and used over and over again.

Copy the

Using the picture below, grab your colouring pens or pencils and see if you can colour in the big picture to match it!

colours!

© Peyo

The Smurfs in Central Park

NEW YORK CITY

As Clumsy, Smurfette, Brainy, Grouchy and Gutsy fell through the hole, Papa, who was last, spotted a stick and grabbed it in the hope of saving them. But when he looked up he saw the stick was being held by Gargamel.

"Looks like you've got the short end of the stick, eh?" laughed Gargamel. But Papa let go and followed the others through the hole.

The Smurfs emerged in another waterfall in a very similar-looking grotto. The six Smurfs flew through the air and landed on top of each other on a grassy bank. When they saw they were surrounded by rubbish, they realised they weren't anywhere near the Smurf Village!

"Uh… Smurfs," called Clumsy, who had made his way to the top of a small rise. "You may want to take a look at this."

They all climbed the rock to join him and they saw the towering glass, steel and granite skyline surrounding New York's Central Park South.

"Oh, my smurf!" gasped Smurfette.

"Where the smurf are we?" asked Grouchy.

"Up the smurfin' creek without a paddle!" said Gutsy. He pointed at the hole in the waterfall that was closing. "At least they're not coming after us…"

EX-
CIII-
TED!

ANJELOU

But the portal suddenly grew bigger and Azraël came shooting through, closely followed by Gargamel. "Must. Have. Smurfs," he shouted.

The Smurfs headed towards a boathouse, hoping to hide out and circle back to the waterfall once they'd lost Gargamel and the cat. But there was a big party in the building.

It was a press event for Anjelou Cosmetics. Patrick Winslow eased through the crowd, shaking hands, greeting people. He re-arranged a couple of female models so that the products they were showing off could be seen more easily.

His boss, Odile Anjelou, the owner of the cosmetics company, was talking to a reporter from Fox5 News. When Patrick approached her, she announced loudly that he was now the Vice President of Marketing.

"You fired Ralph?" he asked, amazed.

"His campaign was rubbish," complained Odile. "He gave me what I asked for, not what I want. Can you give me what I want? I need you to create a new campaign for Jouvenal. It can be ready for the launch..."

"Odile, the launch is two days away," said Patrick, exasperated.

"Is that going to be a problem?"

"No. I mean, God only needed six days for the whole world, right?" said Patrick.

"Fail me," warned Odile, "and maybe you can work for Him." She walked off leaving Patrick stunned.

Just before he left the event a little later, Patrick went back into the building for one more Anejelou box, as an assistant called a cab for him.

Meanwhile, the Smurfs gazed out across a lake to the waterfall. The hole had now completely closed, but Papa believed there would be another blue moon and the portal would open again.

"Let's take shelter until dark," he suggested.

Azraël had caught up with them and as they again ran away the cat caught a mouthful of Smurfette's hair in his mouth. He thought she would be easy prey...

Clumsy accidentally fell into one of Patrick's boxes as he tried to run away. And before he could get out another box was thrown on top, trapping him inside.

The other Smurfs watched Patrick carry the boxes to the taxi and, at the last moment, they saw Clumsy's fingers poking out from the bottom of the two boxes. They had to save him!

They ran along tree branches and onto some scaffolding to keep up with the cab. By the time they jumped on to the taxi roof, Gargamel and Azraël were gaining on them.

The cab driver suddenly slammed on his brakes. Gargamel smacked straight into the back of the car.

Gargamel was left stunned on the ground and as the car pulled away an Anjelou business card fluttered free from the cab's bumper.

Gargamel stared at the unusual logo on the card while the Smurfs stared at the sights of New York.

The taxi pulled up at a Manhattan apartment and all of the Smurfs climbed off the roof of the cab onto a tree. Patrick carried the boxes into the seven-storey high building where Grace, his pregnant wife, was waiting.

"Guess what?" asked Patrick.

"They invented zero calorie pizza?" replied Grace. "Ooh, the baby kicked."

Patrick directed the rest of his conversation towards the unborn child. When he revealed the news about the new job his wife was delighted.

"It's provisional," he warned. "If I wow Cruella D'Odile I keep the job. If not, my head goes on the pike next to the last guy. But... I have two days."

"Two days? But that means you'll miss the ultrasound scan of the baby," she said.

Grace was disappointed but she smiled anyway.

Outside, Gargamel and Azraël sat beneath a street light. They'd lost the Smurfs and the wizard wondered how they would find them again. The cat coughed up a hairball that had Smurfette's long hair wrapped around it.

All the wizard needed now was a laboratory so he could test the hair and use magic to find the Smurfs.

In the distance, lights came on and illuminated Belvedere Castle. That would be perfect for Gargamel! As he and Azraël let themselves into the castle cellar, the exhausted Smurfs climbed a fire escape, peering through every apartment window.

Gutsy spotted the box he thought Clumsy had fallen into and the Smurfs crept into the apartment. By the time they reached the box, Clumsy had gone. He was being chased through the apartment by Elway, the Winslow's dog!

Continued on p48

Spot the

Clumsy's lost in New York

Smurfette and Clumsy have lost each other in New York City. Can you find the right path that brings them back together again? Answers on p77.

Start

Finish

A to Z of Smurfs

A B C D E

A is for: Azraël, a flea-bitten cat. Can you think of any more As that rhyme with this one?

B is for: Baker, who Bakes all the bread. And also for Brainy, who has a big head.

C is for: Central, the name of the Park where the Smurfs find themselves lost in the dark.

D is for: Dragon wand, a sinister tool. It belongs to Gargamel, the evil old fool.

E is for: Elway, the Winslows' dog. E is also for Essence, and Enchanted Forest.

F G H I

F is for: Farmer Smurf, not a village life fan. He's more of a fruit and vegetable man.

G is for: Grouchy, Gutsy and Greedy. And for Gargamel who thinks he's a Genius.

H is for: Hairball – ugh, a horrible mess coughed up by Azraël for Gargamel's spell.

I is for: the Invisibility Shield that protects Smurf Village from the outside world.

J K L M

J is for: Jump – just like Clumsy does into the box, where he gets trapped!

K is for: Kick. The baby Kicked Grace. Grouchy Kicked Patrick. A little girl Kicked Patrick too!

L is for: the La La La Song that all the Smurfs sing. Can you think of any more Ls?

M is for: Mushroom, where Papa Smurf lives. Can you think of any more Ms?

Smurfette has been practising her A to Z and tried to come up with something in Smurfland and beyond for each letter. She even managed to make some of them rhyme. Can you help her where she didn't find many?

N O P Q

N is for: the New job that Patrick seems to have won. Can you think of any more Ns?

O is for: Odile, the cosmetics' firm owner. She can be a bit of a moaner.

P is for: Papa Smurf, the wisest and oldest of Smurfs. P is also for Potion.

Q is for: Quill, an old pen that Papa uses to write out spells. Can you think of any more Qs?

R S T U V

R is for: Ralph, Patrick's poor predecessor. Also for Ron, Patrick's assistant.

S is for: Smurfette and also for Shadow. Can you think of any more Ss?

T is for: the Toilet Paper that Clumsy got all Tied up in. Can you think of any more Ts?

U is for: the Umbrella Patrick used to attack the Smurfs. Can you think of any more Us?

V is for: Vice President of Marketing, Patrick's new job.

W X Y Z

W is for: the Waterfall in the Enchanted Forest. Can you think of any more Ws?

X is for: eXcited, eliXir, eXcellent, and in taXi. Can you think of more words containing X?

Y is for: Yowl, the noise Azraël makes to alert his owner to anything.

Z is for: the Zero calorie pizza that pregnant Grace was craving for!

The Winslows
and the Smurfs

While Papa and the other Smurfs were looking in the empty box for Clumsy, Clumsy was elsewhere in the apartment hiding from the dog, Elway.

He'd found his way to the bathroom, but Elway was scratching and barking at the door trying to get in. Clumsy tried to hide in the basin and stupidly ate a mouthful of soap, then he fell into the toilet and got tied up in a load of toilet paper as he tried to escape!

NEW
YORK
CITY

Patrick was working at his laptop but was restless and kept wandering in to the living room where he had left the boxes.

Grace was woken by the dog's scratching and barking. When she opened the bathroom door and saw the soggy paper inside the toilet bowl she thought Elway had created the mess. She used a toilet brush to fish out the paper, but just as she was about to throw it way, the mess started to wiggle!

When Clumsy popped his head up, Grace screamed. Then Clumsy screamed! Patrick opened one of the boxes in the living room and five Smurfs jumped out. Patrick screamed. The Smurfs screamed!

Grace flung Clumsy across the room. The Smurfs ran out of the living room to rescue Clumsy. Grouchy stopped for a second by Patrick, who had fallen over in shock, and kicked him in the chin.

"This is for Clumsy," said Grouchy.

Patrick warned Grace that they were under attack, but she walked into the living room cuddling Clumsy. She told Patrick that they were friendly creatures, but he needed a bit more convincing.

Over at Belvedere Castle, Gargamel concocted his little potion that would help him find the Smurfs. He wore a ring that would carry the essence until he needed it.

Back in the Winslows' kitchen the Smurfs were singing the La La La Song. Patrick was still freaked out but Grace thought that little blue people singing in her kitchen was crazy and delightful.

Eventually Patrick was won over by the Smurfs who explained they needed a new blue moon so they could open the hole back to the Enchanted Forest.

NEW YORK CITY

BEHOLD THE AWESOME POWER OF ME

Patrick searched on his laptop to find when the next blue moon was due and told Papa Smurf.

But Papa also needed a stargazer so that he could check the right star alignment too.

Papa thought the computer was a magic window, and that the picture of the blue moon was saved onto the machine.

The next morning
Gargamel and Azraël
walked the streets looking
for Smurfs. Grace got ready for
her ultrasound appointment. Patrick
got ready for work.

The Smurfs wanted to go to work
with Patrick. They didn't realise he had
to predict himself what cosmetics people
might want to buy! They thought he had a
fortune teller at work!

Clumsy was left behind so that he
didn't cause any trouble, and the rest of
the Smurfs hitched a ride on the roof of
Patrick's cab.

He only noticed the Smurfs when
he arrived at work, so he hid them inside
his coat where they tickled him and
made him laugh.

Upstairs at Anjelou headquarters, Odile was not impressed when Patrick wriggled and laughed as she spoke to him. She didn't realise he was being tickled.

In the privacy of Patrick's office, the Smurfs were allowed out, but they drove him mad because they insisted on singing the La La La Song as he tried to work. They sang the song all the time back home at Smurf Village!

Gargamel arrived on Fifth Avenue and recognised the logo on the Anjelou building. It was the same as the logo on the business card he'd picked up the day before.

He went inside and found Odile demonstrating some anti-wrinkle cream on the face of an older woman, who turned out to be her mother.

Gargamel pointed out that Odile's "potion" hadn't worked very well! Just to show everyone how good he was at spells, he made the woman's wrinkles disappear.

The woman looked 25 years younger – but Gargamel had used all of the essence he'd extracted from Smurfette's hair!

The Smurfs had wreaked havoc in Patrick's office so he called Grace and asked her to come and collect them.

She and the Smurfs were almost back at the apartment when the taxi pulled up at a red traffic light and Gutsy noticed, through the car window, a picture of a telescope in a store window.

Papa had said he needed a stargazer to help them get home – and there it was! While the taxi was at a standstill, the Smurfs jumped out and dashed through the traffic towards the store.

Grace had to pay the driver and follow them. She called Patrick to ask him to come and help her...

Patrick was on his way out of the Anjelou building when Gargamel bumped into him. Azraël recognised Patrick as the Smurf thief!

The evil pair chased after Patrick who was heading to the world-famous FAO Schwarz store where the Smurfs were looking for their stargazer. The little blue beings were all over the place, on different floors, in different departments.

A child picked up Clumsy thinking he was a doll, and she wanted to buy him...

Continued on p64

Brainy's challenge

Brainy thinks he's so clever! He's jumbled up these names to see how quickly you can put the letters in the right order again.
Answers on p77.

1. CHEAT LAZE ART

_ _ _ _ _ _ _ _ _ _ _ _ _

2. A HAZED TAM WRIGGLER

_ _ _ _ _ _ _ _ _ _ _ _ _ _ _ _ _ _

3. FEE MRS TUT

_ _ _ _ _ _ _ _ _

4. PLASTIC WINK ROW

_ _ _ _ _ _ _ _ _ _ _ _ _ _

5. CRY GO UH

_ _ _ _ _ _ _

6. A FARMS PUP

_ _ _ _ _ _ _ _ _

7. ALOUD LEE JOIN

_ _ _ _ _ _ _ _ _ _ _ _

8. CUM SLY

_ _ _ _ _ _

9. RGECA

_ _ _ _ _

10. UGYTS

_ _ _ _ _

Where are the Smurfs?

Can you find the Smurfs hiding in this picture? There are TEN altogether. Circle them as you spot them.
Answers on p78.

Match the Pairs

Which of these pictures match exactly, and which are the odd ones out? Draw a line between the ones that match and a circle around the ones that dont.

Answers on p77.

C

D

3

4

Try to avoid being caught by Gargamel! Use a dice and counters to play this game with friends. Everyone should throw the dice first, and the one with the highest score goes first. If you land on a square with Papa at the bottom of a ladder, you climb up the ladder. If you land on a square containing Gargamel, you slide down the Dragon Wand.

20

19

18

15

16

17

Miss a Turn

8

7

Throw Again

6

3

4

5

Remove this circle to
hang on door.

Ma Sm door h

STOP

Let everyone know
when they can come
in to your room, or
if they have to keep
out, by making a
funky door hanger
like this one.

Either trace the
pictures onto card,
scan them to a
computer, copy the
drawings and colour
them in, or cut these
ones out and paste
them onto two sides
of a piece of card.
Cut the card to shape.

Ask an adult for help
with scissors.

Smurf Chaos

While Grouchy searched the store for the stargazer, he was startled by an electronic owl.

He stumbled and fell into a vat of small blue sweets. Not knowing what they were, he initially thought they were Smurf droppings! Then he realised they were in his mouth… and tasted quite nice.

He overdosed on the chocolate sweets and found himself chatting up a green doll. But she didn't respond…

While Gargamel was chasing Patrick, the wizard noticed the display of the blue sweets in a shop window. He also spotted Grouchy, who was now on a serious sugar high!

"Don't ever forget," Grouchy said tearfully to the doll, "that for one magical moment, our two worlds met. And I wasn't grouchy. I wasn't. Can you just say one thing? Please! I'm dying here..."

Gargamel sucked the Smurf up into a leaf vacuum he had found in the store. "That's one!" he chuckled.

Patrick rescued Clumsy from the girl that wanted to buy him. "Hey, that's mine!" said the girl.

"I'm sorry, little girl," apologised Patrick, "but this one's not for sale."

The girl kicked him in the shin.

Grace found Smurfette shopping for a new dress. As she scooped the Smurf into her arms, Smurfette complained, "Wait, I'm shopping!"

"Let's shop later," said Grace.

A bunch of kids spotted Smurfette and thought she was another doll. Grace ran away from them with Smurfette in her hand.

Brainy, Papa and Gutsy had finally found a telescope display but another bunch of children had seen them and thought they were toys.

"Hold onto your knickers, boys," shouted Gutsy. "It's about to get grizzly."

"Just hang onto that stargazer," pleaded Papa.

The Smurfs fell off the display and landed on a skateboard, along with the telescope they had grabbed. As they hurtled through the store, Gargamel appeared with his leaf vacuum. Only Papa escaped, still on the skateboard.

"Two more!" whooped Gargamel, just as he saw Grace coming towards him.

Azraël had spotted Smurfette peeping out of Grace's bag and he leapt onto her, knocking the bag to the floor. Smurfette escaped, only to run right into Gargamel and his leaf vacuum.

Gargamel aimed the hose at her just as Papa sailed by on the skateboard and rescued her.

Instead of a Smurf, Gargamel sucked up his own cat! Azraël was stuck.

"Let me help you with that," said Patrick, who had appeared behind Gargamel. He flipped the switch from suck to blow. Azraël shot out – followed by Brainy, Gutsy and Grouchy. And a lot of leaves.

Patrick collected all of the Smurfs while Grace went to pay for the telescope. As they left the store Gargamel, still battling with the blowing leaves, was arrested by the police and for stealing a leaf vacuum!

Back at the apartment Papa set up the telescope while Patrick completed his advertising campaign.

Patrick would have liked to have been adventurous and gone with the Blue Moon imagery but decided to play safe and go with a more regular campaign.

All he had to do was press SEND and it would appear on billboards the following morning.

But Patrick was distracted by the Smurfs as they played on a music-making game on the television.

Clumsy was on Patrick's desk and in the excitement he fell and landed on the laptop keyboard. He managed to switch the ads by accident, from the safe option back to the Smurf-inspired Blue Moon campaign.

Papa announced that the Smurfs could go home soon, just not tonight.

In jail, Gargamel bewitched a little moth. "Oh, you and I are kindred spirits little one," he whispered.

"Both of us meant to soar. Go now and bring back an army of mighty eagles to free me. Fly and bring back your brethren. Fly... fly... fly!"

The next morning, as Gargamel was about to be beaten by a fellow inmate, a giant flock of flies swarmed around the wizard to rescue him. "Flies? Flies?" he yelled at the moth. "I said 'Fly! Fly!' Not 'flies', you light-loving moron!"

Eventually the flies rescued him and returned him to Belvedere Castle.

Meanwhile, back at the Winslows' apartment Papa was excited.

"Great news!" he said. "The stars have revealed the perfect time to Smurf the Blue Moon! It has to be done tonight, between first star and high moon.

"But we'll need a magic spell that works in this realm to open the portal that will return us home."

Patrick remembered a shop that sold antique books. Papa thought the spell he needed might be found there.

In the middle of a smurf hug, they suddenly noticed Patrick's Blue Moon advert on a billboard opposite. Realising he'd probably be sacked now, Patrick dashed into his office to see how that image had been sent.

As he headed to work a message arrived on his phone.

"Fix this," it said, "or you're FIRED! Odile."

On his way to work he saw all the billboards were showing the Blue Moon advert. He reached in to his pocket for his phone and instead pulled out an ultrasound picture of the baby.

Gargamel reached Belvedere Castle and found the last drop of Smurf essence he'd created, there was only a tiny amount at the bottom of the tube. He'd used the rest of it on the anti-wrinkle magic for Odile's mother.

Using a sat-nav and the subway, five of the Smurfs found their way to the shop that sold the books of spells. Clumsy had stayed behind again.

Not far away, Gargamel was told by a tramp that little blue people had gone into the book store. Gargamel reached the Smurfs just as Papa finished copying the incantation with a quill and ink.

"All that remains now," said Papa, "is to return to the waterfall and invoke this spell. Tonight. And we can go home."

"Oh, you're going home? All right …" It was the wizard with his cat. "To a little place I like to call BellVeeduray Castle, where your essence shall finally be mine."

He pointed his dragon wand at the cowering group who then scattered. Gargamel cast his spell but as the bolt of blue energy rocketed towards the Smurfs, Papa used an old Feng Shui mirror to deflect it, first at Azraël and then at Gargamel, who crashed into a bookshelf.

Papa gave the spell to Brainy. "Brainy, take the spell. Brew the potion and smurf the moon tonight. It has to be tonight! No matter what happens," he ordered. "Do not come back for me."

As the Smurfs made good their escape, Papa turned to face Gargamel, who kept throwing spells at Papa which froze the Smurf in mid-air.

"Papa! Noooo!" screamed Smurfette, peering through a grate in the drain they'd all run down.

"Just go!" said Papa.

"Keep moving lads. Do as Papa said," ordered Gutsy pulling Smurfette down into the pipe with them.

"Papa told us to smurf the moon and that's exactly what we're gonna do."

At the waterfall Brainy said the incantation over a boiling kitchen pot perched on a camping stove. Just as the blue smoke erupted from Brainy's potion, blue tendrils shot into the sky and turned the moon blue.

"I did it," said Brainy, who had contacted Papa with a mobile phone.

Everyone in New York saw the blue moon, including Odile and her guests at the Jouvenal launch party.

"It's the Anjelou moon," said one partygoer.

Patrick, Grace and the Smurfs reached Belvedere Castle just as Brainy showed up with all the Smurfs from Smurf Village.

"I went home and got a few friends," Brainy yelled.

The Smurfs hitched a ride on the back of some pigeons to get Clumsy.

Patrick arrived back at the apartment before they did and took a call from Odile. He convinced her to consider his Once in a Blue Moon magical campaign. When the Smurfs arrived they told Patrick, Grace and Clumsy that Gargamel had Papa in a place called BellVeedaRay Castle. Patrick knew they meant Belvedere. They sent Brainy to the waterfall and went to save Papa.

There was a huge battle, and the Smurfs finally grabbed Gargamel's dragon wand and turned his own evil magic onto the wizard.

Papa had learned a lesson, though. Instead of trusting in Clumsy, Papa had trusted in a vision that hadn't worked properly.

The Smurfs made their way back through the portal at the waterfall.

Brainy, Grouchy and Gutsy and Smurfette said their goodbyes to Grace and Patrick.

Grace told Clumsy that he was her hero. Then, at last, it was Papa's turn.

"Well, Master Winslow – thank you. You saved me. You saved my whole family," thanked Papa.

"Actually," said Patrick, "I think it was the other way around."

And so the Smurfs left the strange city. They left it a little sweeter, a little wiser, and a little smurfier.

As the portal closed for the last time, Odile called Patrick to thank him for giving her what she wanted.

She didn't sack him. The Blue Moon campaign was a success.

THE END

Clumsy's Quiz

1
Which two Smurfs did Clumsy accidentally hit?

a) Grouchy & Gutsy
b) Smurfette & Papa
c) Brainy & Farmer

2
What is the name of the waterfall where the portal opens?

a) Smurf Falls
b) Niagara Falls
c) The Forbidden Falls

3
Where did the Smurfs hide until they could circle back to the portal?

a) a boathouse
b) in the water
c) a Wendy house

4
What protects Smurf Village from the outside the world?

a) a big bouncer
b) an invisibility shield
c) an evil wizard

5
On what did Greedy and Farmer Smurf ride to collect smurfberries?

a) Farmer Smurf's tractor
b) a bicycle
c) storks

6
What does Gargamel need from the Smurfs?

a) their happy blue essence
b) lots of love and friendliness
c) their village

7
What time of year is it in Smurf Village?

a) Christmas
b) Blue Moon Time
c) Summer

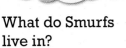

8

What do Smurfs live in?

a) houses
b) trees
c) mushrooms

9

Why did Clumsy need the smurfroot?

a) to eat
b) to make mud packs
c) because he likes it

10

How long does Patrick have to launch his new campaign?

a) two days
b) as long as it takes
c) two weeks

11

What did Patrick use to attack the Smurfs with?

a) a loofah
b) an umbrella
c) a sword

12

What do the Smurfs call a telescope?

a) a telescope
b) a stargazer
c) a moon viewing thing

13

Grouchy thought the blue sweets were what?

a) candy
b) chocolate
c) Smurf droppings

14

Who does Gargamel ask to help free him from jail?

a) a moth
b) a fellow inmate
c) Patrick

15

Which is your favourite Smurf?

a) Smurfette
b) Clumsy
c) Gutsy

Answers on p77

73

Brainey
Dot-to

Can you join the
dots on these
pictures of Brainy
and Papa?

and Papa
-Dot

When you have
finished, colour
the two pictures
in using coloured
pens or pencils.

Answers

Page 10: Odd One Out!
Number 5

Page 11: Shadow Smurfs
Number 9

Page 20: Brainy's Quiz
1. Gutsy, 2. 542,
3. To cause trouble amongst the Smurfs, 4. Brainy, 5. Gold,
6. A nasty, sneaky, hypocritical wizard,
7. He used his knowledge and alchemy to transform her,
8. A flea-bitten cat, 9. Blue Moon, 10. Because he always ends up causing an accident,
11. Fox 5,
12. Patrick Winslow,
13. Anjelou Cosmetics,
14. Odile Anjelou, 15. Through a portal, 16. Six, 17. 31,
18. Cruella DOdile,
19. Because he had Clumsy in a box, 20. Belvedere.

Page 22: Jigsaw Fix
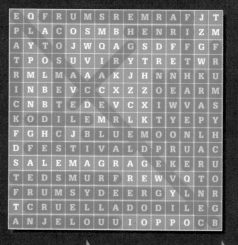

Page 24: Brainy Crossword

	S	M	U	R	F	E	T	T	E				
	T				N								
	O				C	A	B						
S	M	U	R	F									
	K				B	O	A	T	H	O	U	S	E
	S				H				M				
	A		F	O	R	E	S	T		B	L	U	E
	Z				P				R				
	R	O	O	T					F				
	A			A					S				
	E			L									
	L												

Page 25: Papas Wordsearch

E	Q	F	R	U	M	S	R	E	M	R	A	F	J	T
P	L	A	C	O	S	M	B	H	E	N	R	I	Z	M
A	Y	T	O	J	W	Q	A	G	S	D	F	F	G	F
T	P	O	S	U	V	I	R	Y	T	R	E	T	W	R
R	M	L	M	A	A	A	K	J	H	N	N	H	K	U
I	N	B	E	V	C	C	X	Z	Z	O	E	A	R	M
C	N	B	T	E	D	E	V	C	X	I	W	V	A	S
K	O	D	I	L	E	M	R	L	K	T	Y	E	P	Y
F	G	H	C	J	B	L	U	E	M	O	O	N	L	H
D	F	E	S	T	I	V	A	L	D	P	R	U	A	C
S	A	L	E	M	A	G	R	A	G	E	K	E	R	U
T	E	D	S	M	U	R	F	R	E	W	V	Q	T	O
F	R	U	M	S	Y	D	E	E	R	G	Y	L	N	R
T	C	R	U	E	L	L	A	D	O	D	I	L	E	G
A	N	J	E	L	O	U	U	I	O	P	P	O	C	B